LET LOVE

COME LAST

LET LOVE COME LAST

BY

TAYLOR CALDWELL

"Let love come last, after the lesson's learned;
Like all things else, love also must be earned."

NEW YORK
CHARLES SCRIBNER'S SONS

The characters and events in this novel are fictitious.
Any resemblance to actual persons or events is coincidental. If the name of any actual person has been given
to any character it was unintentional and accidental.

This book is dedicated with compassion to all who
are parents and to all who hope to be

LET LOVE
COME LAST

EPILOGUE

"—My dear and beloved Children—"

The words had a grave resonance, like the opening of the funeral Mass, like the organ sound of limitless mourning and the last murmur of futile tragedy. They were an epilogue to a man's life, thought Ursula Prescott, her bent head throwing a shadow upon the paper in her hands. But then, was there ever prologue or epilogue? In the beginning the end was already inherent; one might almost say it was simultaneous.

Ursula's fine and delicate hand touched the paper gently. She was not a woman who cried easily. She was not really crying now; she knew this. Not crying as a woman often cries, copiously and emotionally, and with a bursting relief.

She folded the paper slowly, but not before she had again read the two terse words: "—my wife." Those words struck her with fresh suffering for a moment. Then she said aloud, as a mother would say to a tormented child who at last begs for forgiveness: "Yes, yes, my darling. I understand. It doesn't matter." Nothing mattered, but that William might have peace. She had never been a religious woman. She had hoped, at one time, for personal immortality. But now, almost with passion, she hoped that William had found complete annihilation, complete darkness and nothingness.

She stood up, went to the somber casement windows, and glanced out. The small private park swept before her, darkening steadily under the dark opal of a winter sky. The naked black trees were daubed with snow; the ground glimmered spectrally. Far off, she could just see the low gray wall that surrounded the grounds. Beyond them, the street lamps burned with a fugitive and blowing yellow. How often, through how many years, she had stood at this window, and had seen this exact scene, and had felt its desolation! She had hated it, for she had found something inimical in the sight, just as she had found something inimical in this house which she was leaving forever in less than an hour. She had always hated this huge and echoing house, dark and forbidding in its long narrow corridors, its false turrets and towers of swart and heavy stone, its grim walls and slits of high windows.

Her thoughts ran on. She thought of Oliver, who would be coming with Barbara very soon, in that horrible bright-red automobile which they had just purchased, and of which they were inordinately proud. Involuntarily, and with sadness, she smiled. But the loud thunder and roar of the automobile would be a pleasant sound to her now, for all its stink of gasoline, and its smoke. Oliver, she thought.

Ursula pressed her aching forehead against the cold leaded window. She strained for a first glimpse of the vivid red monster which would carry her away from this house forever. Behind her lay shrouded rooms, with only a single light burning far down in the entrance hall. The servants had all been dismissed. She was alone in this mansion, where four of her children had been born, and where William had died. She could hear the dull booming of vagrant echoes, which were not the echoes of anything living. The room in which she stood, her bedroom, was growing cold; the fire had died down to a heap of ash and sparks.

Dear, dear Oliver. Had it not been for Oliver, this last night in this dreadful house would have been the most final of despairs.

Restlessly, out of her intense weariness, Ursula walked back and forth before the great casement windows, watching for Oliver, listening for the sound of his bright infernal machine. She passed the table where she had laid the paper. She put her hand over it, quickly, protectingly. "Yes, dear," she said, aloud, very gently, and as if comforting.

The great house boomed and creaked. She had a vision of its many rooms, shuttered and arctic, the mirrors and the immense furniture covered with dust cloths. She saw again the white, the dark-blue, the brown, marble fireplaces, before which she would never stand again. She shivered.

She heard a loud and staccato series of explosions. She turned to the window again. A pair of fiery eyes were rushing up the broad driveway. Oliver and Barbara had arrived for her. They would rescue her, and take her away.

It would be a beginning again. Not the beginning of youth, with joy and anticipation. It was only the beginning of age. For her, however, it would, perhaps, also be the beginning of peace.

PART ONE

"Let parents, then, bequeath to their children not riches, but the spirit of reverence."

PLATO

CHAPTER I

IF ALL her life had indeed been complete from the first drawing of her breath, Ursula, in later years, often thought that a kind of beginning had taken place on a cool white twilight in late March, 1879, in the city where she had been born—Andersburg.

Andersburg was never to grow larger than one hundred thousand souls. In 1879, it boasted a population of fifty thousand. There had been no impetus for any enormous growth, for Pittsburgh was less than one hundred miles away. Foothills, covered with fine forests (much of it first-growth timber), gave it a natural beauty, and even endowed it with the reputation of being an excellent summer resort for those curious creatures who must often fly from their fellowmen lest they kill them in a moment of frenzy, or of complete understanding. Even in 1879, many "lodges" had been built in the foothills, summer homes of refugees from New York, Philadelphia, Pittsburgh, and even of Bostonians who were tired of the quaint New England countryside. New England eyes automatically expected to see the clean white steeples, set among neat severe houses and gardens, to which they were accustomed. But even seen from the hills, Andersburg had a sprawling and untidy character, a burliness of brown stone, and its houses had an air of heavy crudeness and stolidity. The city was not too far from rich coal fields, and many of the owners lived here in mansions indescribably ugly and formless, but very opulent.

Andersburg had a very small middle class, composed of small manufacturers, shopkeepers, wholesalers, merchants, bankers, lawyers, doctors and teachers. It was a smug and tight middle class, though it had little money. In compensation, it invented prestige, and affected, on the one hand, to despise the workers, whom it feared, and, on the other, pretended to laugh at the rich "outsiders" who drew their fortunes from coal and oil and rents and land.

Ursula Wende's father had been a teacher in the small private school in Andersburg; he had also been a philosopher. "There are only two ways a teacher can escape mass-murdering his pupils," he had once said. "He can acquire a healthy hatred for them, or he can become a philosopher about them."

His pupils came, almost without exception, from the middle-class families. He acquired a philosophy about the middle class, also. He did not go so far as Aristotle in his admiration of this class, but he did believe, sincerely, that their survival was distinctly necessary to the survival of a nation. "As they are without imagination," he would say, "they often smite, like a good sound club, on the delirious brains of fanatics and malignant idealists who would destroy any order for the mere love of anarchy. And they serve another harmless purpose: they furnish material for writers; they are the straw-men who can safely be knocked about by lunatics with missions, without harm either to themselves or to society in general."

August Wende had come of a sound "Pennsylvania Dutch" family, and as he was not completely free from affectation himself, he affected to find his antecedents "amusing" and rather base. But, in truth, they had been a people remarkable for solid common sense and shrewdness, and with a respect for learning which August had found "pitiful." Pitiful or not, their square and sturdy homes had been filled with books and musical instruments, much talk of Schiller and Goethe, much disgusted argument about Bismarck, and much delicate mysticism.

Much of the family fortune had been lost during the war, and when August died, in June 1878, he left his daughter a small fieldstone house in Andersburg, a large plot of uncultivated land just beyond the suburbs to the west, eight thousand dollars in cash, many objets d'art, and multitudinous books. There was nothing else, unless one also added a fine capacity for self-understanding, a clarified serenity of mind, pride, reasonableness, and a balanced ability to observe the world and its doings without overmuch heat.

"I suppose, my love, that you'll have to become a teacher yourself now," he had remarked on his deathbed, with regret. "You will need to remember one thing, and remember it always: Nothing very singular ever turns up anywhere. Consequently, one should never become excited, either over a strange student or a strange event. For there is nothing strange, and, really, nothing very interesting, in all the world."

Even in the moment of her deepest grief, as Ursula had looked down upon her father slowly dying, she had thought: "He is really dying of ennui." For some weeks after his death, she felt that his ennui had had in it elements of tragedy, and so, a certain splendor.

Eight thousand dollars, even when augmented to ten thousand dollars after the sale of some of the objets d'art, would not last her a lifetime. She was twenty-seven years old, a "confirmed" spinster. Fortunately, she had no relatives to support. Her mother had died when she, herself, had been a child of ten. She was comparatively healthy.

She did not particularly dislike her fellowmen, so that she contemplated teaching with no aversion. Though August Wende had made fun of his parents' thriftiness, he had been exceedingly thrifty himself, and Ursula was a competent and frugal housewife, a bargainer in the food shops and the clothing establishments. As she had always made her own clothing, she was a clever dressmaker and milliner. She had, therefore, three choices of a way of making a comfortable living. She did not consider teaching better than either of the others, for she was without false pride. She decided to take some months or even years to consider. Teaching had "prestige," to which she was indifferent, but dressmaking and millinery might bring in more money.

She went alone, scandalously, to New York, enjoyed a few operas and plays, walked endlessly, studied the bonnets in the fine shops, and the rich gowns, garnered many ideas and much refreshment, and returned home in calm and rejuvenated spirits. She worked in her pretty garden all summer, preserved jams and jellies in the autumn, made handsome frocks of the materials she had purchased in New York, through the winter, set her garden in the spring. Then she began to think of what she must do for a living. Her capital was sacred. That must never be touched. She knew her ideas were middle-class, and was proud of them.

Once, in her early twenties, she had considered marriage. But though she had attracted a number of young men, she had never been overly attracted to them in turn. She had had a happy and tranquil life with her father, and, as she was a keen observer, she had not believed the marriage state, as exemplified among her friends, to be particularly ecstatic, or even satisfying. At twenty-seven, she had only one suitor.

She finally decided that she would accept a teaching post. She had been offered a teaching position in a small, girls' school, with a salary large enough to take care of her very modest requirements. This, then, was the best way open to her.

The small fieldstone house, set on a quiet tree-lined street, had an old loveliness. She would not sell it, though good offers had been made to her. It was her refuge, with its little library full of books, with its excellent old furniture, its three bedrooms with sloping ceilings, its ancient elms and perfect small garden, its leaded windows and strong plank doors, its flagged walks and hedges, its good paintings of plump ancestors on the panelled walls. Both she and her father had had exquisite taste. There was not an ugly or a cheap note either in the house or in its grounds. Her front windows looked on the narrow cobbled street, but the rear windows, from the bedrooms, had a view of the distant lavender foothills, and of the gardens.

Here Ursula could entertain her very few friends, but not too frequently. She was happiest when alone. There was nothing morbid in this. She had the contemplative mind, poised and still and lucid. She did not pretend to dislike people, as August had sometimes pretended. There were moments when she felt quite warm towards her friends.

Now it was March, pale, white, sterile March, with its wan cold twilights and its silences. She would often stand in the wet brown garden, her shawl over her shoulders, and listen for the first sound of life, drawing the chill pure air into her lungs. Nothing, she thought, will ever change. She was not sorry.

Yet on the twenty-eighth of March, with spring definitely established, things changed for her forever. The change came with William Prescott.

The jonquils massed themselves in cold golden pools near the rear wall of the house, strong, watery, and vigorous, shining even in the pale twilight. The wind from the hills ranged over the garden, and it raised a burst of fecund scent, as lustful as a mating animal. The ground had darkened; in the west, over the hills, lay a dull brazen lake, filled with the black rags of approaching clouds. Above the lake stood the slender silver of the moon, a curve of ice glimmering and sharp.

Ursula had not as yet lit a lamp in the house; it waited for her, dark and silent, with a low red fire in the parlor. She was cutting an armful of the jonquils, and thinking, with a tranquil sadness, of her father, who had preferred these flowers above all others. Perhaps it was because, like himself, they had so little perfume. There was nothing heady about them, like the roses, nothing passionate, like the tiger lily, nothing sweet and intense, like the lilac. They pleased the eye; they did not disturb the spirit. They had a simple perfection of petal—and they were soon gone. Ursula sighed. Regretfully, she concluded that her father, after all, had not been even a philosopher.

She would put the jonquils into water tonight, enjoying the mass of them against her walnut walls; tomorrow, she would carry them to his grave. Of course, he was not really in his grave. He was not anywhere. But she would allow herself the brief sentimentality of pretending to believe that he was aware of the jonquils, and of herself. There were times when it was almost soothing to pay lip-service to conventional belief. One or two of her neighbors would see her in the cemetery, and remark on the jonquils, and would think more highly of her for it. Ursula smiled faintly. She did not, truly, particularly care about the opinions of others. But if she were to be commented upon, she preferred that the comments be kind, rather than malicious.

My life is closing in upon me, she reflected. It does not matter. I am an old maid. Even that does not matter. I have a peaceful fire waiting for me, and books, and I have eight thousand dollars in the bank, and no one can disturb me. If I choose to indulge myself in hypocrisy, then I can do so without reproachful eyes fixed upon me.

The curve of the moon brightened, and now the wind became colder. Even the jonquils faded in the darkening twilight. But a white and spectral light hovered in the branches of trees, still bare and waiting.

It was then that she heard the brass knocker sounding loudly on her front door. Echoes bounded back to her. The whole street would hear that peremptory summons. She could not recall that any of her friends were rude enough to sound her knocker so noisily. One did not do that. In this sedate city, still brooding under Quaker traditions, one did not do that.

Annoyed, Ursula thought of heads appearing at windows along the street, staring down at the gray cobblestones and at her door. She entered the house through the rear door, laid the jonquils on the bare scrubbed table in the kitchen, which was lined with knotty pine, thrust a spill into the still glowing coals in the stove, carried the wavering light into the parlor, and there lit a lamp. Whoever stood outside must have seen the warm flare against her undrawn curtains, for he again struck the knocker a resounding blow, impatient and imperious.

Her cat, black and sleek, rose purring from the hearth and rubbed himself against her skirts. She felt the annoyed hardness of her lips, and forced them to part. She laid down her shawl, passed her hands over her hair, went composedly to the door, and opened it to the rush of the dark night air.

The gas-lamps along the street were already flaring in the dusk, yellow and glowing. They outlined the tall broad figure of a man. She could not see his face, only his head, with the hard round hat still upon it. He did not remove his hat for several moments; she could feel his eyes staring down upon her. Then, as if reluctant, he took off his hat, and said, in a cold, quick voice: "Mrs. Wende?"

"Miss," corrected Ursula, as coldly.

There was a ruthless urgency about this stranger, and Ursula had a swift thought that she was glad that she had no relatives who might be ill, no friends whose calamities could really stir and strike her, no fear of any summons to death or suffering. Otherwise, facing this stranger, she might have been alarmed. Now she could observe him on her own invulnerable threshold, and feel only irritation at his brusqueness.

"What is it you wish?" she asked. She had a clear, chill voice, the voice of a born spinster, as she had often wryly commented to herself.

"Miss Wende," said the stranger. He paused. He was trying to be polite, she saw. Then he went on: "You have a plot of land, fifteen acres, to the west of the town. I want to buy it. What is your price? I understand it is for sale. Someone told me an hour ago."

Ursula wanted to laugh. But she was still exasperated. Her first impulse was to say: "The land is not for sale," and then shut the door with finality. Yet that was absurd. She wished to sell the land; she had a price already fixed. Mere pique must not do her out of a sale, no matter how she disliked boors.

She said, closing the door a trifle: "You must see my lawyer. He manages all my affairs. Mr. Albert Jenkins, in the Imperial Bank Building, on Landmeer Street."

She saw that discreet heads were already bobbing at the windows of the nearest houses. Her door closed even more. "Mr. Albert Jenkins," she repeated, firmly.

"Nonsense," said the stranger. "Why should I wait until tomorrow? I saw the land this evening, and I immediately wanted it. I can't go to bed without having bought it. I don't want to diddle with lawyers. You sound like a sensible woman. Why pay your lawyer the commission?"

"Simply because he is my lawyer," replied Ursula, obdurately.

"If I go to your lawyer," said the stranger, with a most absurd threat in his voice, "I'll offer him five hundred dollars less than he asks, and then you'll pay his commission to boot." He paused. "I suppose I was mistaken. You aren't a sensible woman after all."

"But why does it have to be settled tonight?" asked Ursula, with a sharp edge to her voice. "I can't bargain with you on the doorstep——"

"Then you can invite me in." His own voice softened, as if he were smiling. "I'm harmless, and I'm in a hurry. You don't need to be afraid of me."

"I'm not in the least afraid," said Ursula, with cool impatience. She hesitated. The heads were still at the windows. If she admitted this man, this stranger, the news would be told at breakfast in every house on the street: "Ursula Wende had a male caller last night; she allowed him to enter her house, though she had no female friend with her. Of course, everyone knows that Ursula is the soul of discretion, but still——"

Suddenly, Ursula was sick of discretion. Besides, she was by nature respectful of money. Extra dollars would not harm her in the slightest. The land was worthless. It adjoined no farms; it was in the least fashionable of the suburbs, and no one wanted it for new houses. She resented the taxes she had to pay on it, small as they were. She thought of the grasping Mr. Jenkins. She opened the door wider, and said, briefly: "Come in."

The man promptly followed her into her tiny warm hall. She had a moment's nervousness as she closed the door and found herself alone with him. She remembered newspaper stories of lone women murdered in their beds. But I am not in my bed, she thought to herself with faint humor. She restrained a desire to hurry into her parlor and place herself close to the poker near the fireplace. She led the way sedately into the room. The lamp had a heartening light. It revealed the walnut panelling on the walls, the faded Aubusson rug in its blue and rosy tints, the well-polished ancient chests, chairs and tables, the cat on the hearth, the darkened portrait over the mantelpiece, the Chelsea porcelain figurines and ormolu clock below it. It all had an exquisite look of loving care and taste, fastidiousness and elegance.

The stranger stood in the center of the room, and looked frankly about him. He smiled. He had a dark saturnine smile. There was about him an atmosphere of force and ruthlessness. All at once, the parlor seemed to Ursula too dainty, too attenuated, too refined, a woman's room, for all her father had furnished it, had chosen each article from the houses of his deceased relatives.

"A nice room," said the stranger. Ursula eyed him narrowly. Was he making game of her? But she saw, after a moment, and with surprise, that he was sincere. He was admiring the room, and everything in it. To Ursula, this seemed grotesque. He was such a big man. He was neither old nor young. She guessed his age as thirty-two or three.

"I always thought there must be such rooms," said the stranger. "I, myself, though, prefer heavier furniture, and thicker rugs. But I know what is here is very good. Probably priceless." There was a suggestion of a query in his voice. Exasperated again, but just a little amused also, Ursula replied: "I really do not know. Everything here belonged to my father's people. He chose what he wished."

"Old, and priceless," said the man. He was well dressed, in an excellently cut coat of the best black broadcloth and discreetly striped trousers. His waistcoat was of heavy silk. His black cravat boasted a good pearl pin. He carried a fine greatcoat on his arm, and his boots were handmade and brilliant. A malacca cane hung from his other arm. His clothing proclaimed the gentleman. But Ursula, with the instinct of her breeding, knew he was no gentleman.

She felt an unfamiliar curiosity, and studied him with more interest than was usual with her. He had a large but narrow head, with thick, straight, black hair, well-combed and neat. Below it was a knotted forehead, brown as if it had been repeatedly, and vulgarly, exposed to much sun. Eyebrows, thick, unruly and very black, almost met over deep-set and restless gray eyes. His nose was predatory, thin and curved, with flaring nostrils. His wide thin mouth was set tautly; he had a sound hard chin with a deep dimple.

With more and more surprise, Ursula said to herself: He has an eloquent face, and very expressive. I do not know whether I like what it expresses, for I do not know what it is. But though his face is eloquent, it has a quality of earth. How can features be so eloquent of so many things, and yet be so coarse? The coarseness, she decided, with astuteness, must come from some quality of his nature.

"Won't you sit down, Mr.——" she suggested, and hated her voice for its note of primness.

"William Prescott," he said, and sat down, after laying his hat, greatcoat and cane on a nearby sofa. He glanced at the fire, then before she could say anything, or make a move, he was up again, was tossing coals on the red embers, and was vigorously stirring them up. "I hate to be cold," he remarked. "I like heat, plenty of heat. I suppose that is because I was so often cold in my life, and could not get warm."

Nonplussed, Ursula watched him, and listened to him. She sat down, feeling quite numb, and waited until he had seated himself again. He gave her his cold, unfriendly smile; she noticed that he had strong white teeth. He should have made her uneasy. But, on the contrary, the queerest excitement stirred her.

She observed he was studying her candidly. She could see herself through his own eyes. She saw her tall slenderness, her narrow waist and high breasts under the russet wool frock, her thin thighs and neat and narrow feet. She saw the white lace collar at her throat, fastened with her mother's cameo brooch circled with seed pearls, and the white lace at her strong but narrow wrists. A ruby ring sparkled on the ring finger of her right hand. The left was ringless. All at once, she did not know why, she was glad that she had fine white hands with the "philosopher's" prominent knuckles, and fingers that tapered. She had no vanity, and she knew that she was not beautiful. Still, friends had commented upon her long oval face, so smooth and cool and colorless except for the rather inflexible mouth of a pale coral tint. She knew that she had a delicately Roman nose, arched and somewhat arrogant, a nose which had caused her secret tears in her girlhood, when she had compared it with the little retroussé or straight noses of her friends.

Her hair and eyes were faultless, she admitted frankly. The hair was smooth and heavy and waveless, very long and thick, and of a deep russet color, like an oaken leaf in autumn. She had eyes to match. Her father had said they reminded him of the best sherry, for, though aloof, they were liquid and bright, flecked with golden brown, and set in strong russet lashes. Ursula never cared much for passing style. She wore her beautiful hair parted in the middle, over a very high white forehead, and drawn back austerely to a large knot on her nape, with never a curl or a coquettish fringe.

She dressed discreetly, but with taste, and she had about her an unbendingly composed air, sometimes a little stern but invariably self-possessed. Once, her father, feeling more affectionate than usual, had told her she was a great lady, and he speculated, audibly, how such a great lady could have sprung from his sturdy, "Pennsylvania Dutch" ancestry. "There is something Spanish about you, my pet," he had said. Then he had added, with a little malice: "But there is nothing Spanish in your temperament."

She had been pleased. But now the memory disturbed her, made her vaguely resentful. What had her father really known of her, and her potentialities?

William Prescott said, with another of his unpleasant smiles: "You think me precipitous coming like this, hardly two hours after seeing your land?"

Ursula was exasperated at her own emotionalism, and she replied in a cool tone: "It does seem extraordinary. You were not expecting to build on it tonight, were you, Mr. Prescott?"

He laughed suddenly. The laugh was hoarse, and as disagreeable as his smile. "Strange to admit, but in a way I was. I never wait. I've found that everything that is ever accomplished is done by precipitate people."

"I prefer people who take a little thought," said Ursula.

He looked at her, still smiling. His small grey eyes were very penetrating and hard, like bits of stone. "I take plenty of thought. But I do it faster than the average person. When I saw that land, I had not only bought it in my mind, but I had built upon it what I wished, complete to the last detail."

She thought: He is a conceited lout.

He continued: "I have been looking for such a piece of ground. Isolated. Large enough, not too large. And cheap. It is the cheapest suburb of Andersburg."

Ursula was again irritated. "You haven't even asked the price. I am not prepared to sell the land cheaply."

"How much?" he asked. She became aware that there was always a demand in his questions. She began to dislike him more and more. She hesitated. She had placed a price of one thousand five hundred dollars on the land. She said indifferently: "Two thousand dollars."

He stared, then glowered. "Two thousand dollars! That's exorbitant. I could buy a fairly good small farm for that."

Ursula smiled frigidly, but said nothing.

"I had expected to pay no more than one thousand five hundred, at the very most," said Mr. Prescott. "Even that is too much, and you know it. There is nothing around it of any value, and you know that, too. I understand they may even put up workmen's shacks all about it! If they do, you won't get a thousand for the whole fifteen acres."

"Mr. Prescott," said Ursula, formally, "I did not solicit you to buy what I own. You came here yourself."

"But you saw I wanted the infernal land, so you put up the price," he said, with a very nasty inflection in his voice. His words were offensive, yet Ursula, incredulously, saw suddenly that his expression was almost admiring.

"I am not going to argue about prices," she said. "I have given you the price I will take. If you do not wish to pay it—or cannot," she added, with a sudden and subtle awareness that with this she could cut him sharply, "then we need not go on with the discussion."

She saw she was right, for he turned an ugly brick-red. "You know nothing of my financial condition," he said rudely. "You know nothing about me; you never saw me before."

So, he was vulnerable. This made Ursula smile with pleasure.

"You are quite correct, Mr. Prescott." She made her voice haughtily insolent. "Who are you? Are you a stranger to Andersburg?"

Now he glanced away from her, and his mouth tightened. "I was born in Andersburg, Miss Wende. On Clifton Street. But, of course, you know nothing of Clifton Street." He said this with an insolence that surmounted her own.

"Oh, yes," remarked Ursula, with repellent pleasantness, "I know all about Clifton Street. The Ladies Aid of my church makes up Christmas baskets for the unfortunate inhabitants. We also gather up discarded clothing, mend and patch and clean it."

All at once, she was disgusted with herself, for she saw him involuntarily glance down at his rich clothing as though it had turned abruptly to rags. The disagreeable expression went from his face, and was replaced by one so gloomy that she hated herself.

"I'm sorry," she said, with real humility and regret. "I ought not to have said that."

He laughed shortly. "I have that effect on people," he said.

He said this, not with apology, but with a kind of hard bitterness and defiance. Then he added: "I no longer live on Clifton Street, Miss Wende. I am temporarily living in the Imperial Hotel." He watched her closely, then smiled. "You aren't impressed?"

"Should I be? Should I admit that I know that the Imperial Hotel is very expensive?" Her words were unkind, but her voice had become gentle at the last.

"I have the best suite," he said, frankly, and his own voice was almost humorous. His eloquent face expressed amusement at himself, and now it lost its earthy quality and took on a vivid liveliness. "When I was a very young fellow, I promised myself I should have that suite. I worked in the hotel for a while, as a waiter."

He watched her narrowly for a look of disdain. But she was gazing at him with that new gentleness. "How nice that you realized your ambition," she commented. Something warm was spreading in her, something she did not recognize as pity. She had never before really pitied anyone, for she had never cared enough.

"My mother kept a boarding-house on Clifton Street, for the men who worked in the Leslie Carriage Shops," he said. "Of course, this is of no interest to you, Miss Wende, and I don't know why I am telling you this. But I might say that I am a lumber man, now. After I was a waiter, I began to work for the American Lumber Company."

Ursula knew Mr. Chauncey Arnold, president of the American Lumber Company. The acquaintanceship was distant, for Ursula had always considered Mr. Arnold to be very gross. The gentleman had tried to cultivate August Wende, without notable success.

"I shan't bore you with all the details," said William Prescott. "Ladies, I know, are not interested in commerce, or money. Except when they try to get the highest price for a poor piece of land," he added, smiling.

Ursula returned the smile. "Mr. Prescott, I'll bore you with a few details of my own. I am an unmarried woman. My father came of a wealthy 'burgher' family, but they lost their money after the war. My father was a schoolmaster. He died less than a year ago. He left me a sum of money, but it is not enough to keep me for the rest of my life. I have found a position as a teacher. The salary is small, even if just enough for my needs. I like to think that I have a small, secure principal. I am quite healthy, and may live a long time. You are, obviously, a gentleman of means. You will forgive me, then, for driving as good a bargain as I can."

She was amazed at her unique retreat from habitual reserve.

She added, with angry pride: "I originally put a price of one thousand five hundred dollars on the land. You may have it for that, if you wish."

He looked down at his big thin hands, brown and strong, and he was thoughtful. "I'll take your original offer of two thousand," he said.

Ursula could not endure this. She stood up. He raised his eyes to her. Then, apparently, he remembered that gentlemen rise when ladies rise, and he, too, stood up. They faced each other on the hearth.

"Mr. Prescott," said Ursula, "my price is one thousand five hundred. I shall take no more. So, let us end the matter."

He inclined his head indulgently, after a moment's study of her. "One thousand five hundred, then." He put his hand in the inner pocket of his coat and drew out a purse of the best Florentine leather and workmanship. His fingers rubbed it almost lovingly. "I will give you a deposit, now, of two hundred, and take your receipt. Within a few days, you can give me the deed, and receive the balance of the money." He looked at her steadily. "Or shall I call on Mr. Jenkins?"

Ursula, for all her irritation, could not help laughing.

"Never mind Mr. Jenkins," she replied. "As you said before, why should I pay him a commission? Only last week he told me that I would never sell that piece of property."

Smiling in answer, William Prescott extended two gold-backed bills to her. She took them. Her fingers brushed his, and a strange thrill ran down her arm, struck at her heart. This so bemused her that she stood there, staring at him in confusion.

"I'll give you a receipt at once," she stammered. She stepped back a single pace; she could not look away from him. He said nothing, but now his eyes were keener than ever. He was frowning, as if disturbed.

She turned suddenly, and went to her delicate rosewood desk in a distant corner of the room. She sat down quickly. Now her eyes blurred. She began to fumble in the drawers of the desk.

She heard his voice beside her. "Let me light the lamp for you," he was saying. He had taken a box of matches from his pocket. He took the chimney off the desk lamp, then lighted it. The little flare trembled as if a breeze had touched it. He had some difficulty with the flame of the lamp. She watched him, as if in a dream, her mouth parted. Then he replaced the chimney. "There now," he said, with absurd triumph, as though he had accomplished something of tremendous difficulty and importance.

She wrote out the receipt. Involuntarily, she managed to brush his fingers again. They looked at each other, hypnotized, as he folded the receipt without glancing at it, and put it away in that resplendent purse. She sat there, and he stood there, for a long time, in utter silence.

He said, in a stupid tone, dull and shaken: "You ought to have gas in this house. It isn't very expensive. And quite safe. I have gas-lights in my suite. Very convenient. Much better light, too, and better for the eyes. Some people object to the glare, and say the smell is more offensive than that of oil. I don't think so. Of course, one has to keep a window a little open. The fumes, you know."

"I've heard about the fumes," said Ursula, faintly, leaning back in her chair. "I understand they give you a headache. I don't think I should care for gas."

"But you must have gas!" cried William Prescott. He appeared quite excited. "One should progress." Then he fell into silence. He stared down at Ursula. The smooth, cool pallor of her face was suffused. She was beautiful as she had never been beautiful before. The light brightened her russet hair to a ring of gold about her head. She felt a warm swelling in her breast, a richness in her thighs, an urgency all through her body.

He turned abruptly and went back to the hearth, and stood there, looking at the fire. Slowly, Ursula got to her feet. She returned to the hearth, sat down. They both stared intensely at the leaping flames that crackled all over the fresh coal. William Prescott, though standing too near her, did not move. There was a somberness about him, and something like a deep silent anger. She could feel this. But she was not alarmed, or dismayed. Something excited rose in her. For the first time since her childhood she was feeling, and not thinking, and the experience was primordial.

The delicate ormolu clock between the Chelsea figurines chimed a sweet clear note in the silence. William Prescott actually started a little. He said, in his strange dull voice: "It is nine. I must be going." He turned away to the sofa, picked up his greatcoat, hat and cane.

Ursula rose. "Yes," she said, dimly, "it is nine o'clock." Something was beating strongly in her throat. "May I ask, Mr. Prescott, what you are going to build on that land? A mill?"

He paused. He did not look at her. There was a cold brutality in his manner. "Why? Does it annoy you that I might build a mill? What have you against mills, Miss Wende?"

"I have nothing against mills!" she cried, with asperity. "Why should I? It's your land, now. Do what you want with it." It was stupid to be trembling like this, as if she were afraid.

"I have no objection to telling you," he said. "I am going to build a house upon it. The biggest house in Andersburg."

It was worse than stupid to experience such a sick shock, thought Ursula confusedly. It was surely nothing to her that he was building a house! But when one built a house, one had a wife, or intended to have one very shortly.

"Mrs. Prescott will be pleased, then," she murmured. She rested her hand against the mantelpiece. I feel quite odd, she thought. I must have gotten a chill, standing so long in the garden.

William Prescott put on his coat before answering. Then he said, with hard denial: "There is no Mrs. Prescott. I am not married."

"I see," said Ursula, in the most imbecile way.

William Prescott's loud voice filled the room: "I want the house for myself! I want room after room, storey after storey! I am going to fill every corner! I am going to have what I've always wanted, and be damned to everybody!"

Ursula was silent.

"If and when I marry, the woman won't matter in the least," said this peculiar man. He looked at her now, almost as if he hated her. "I shall marry only for children. I want to fill my house with children. A woman, to me, has no other reason for existence."

They regarded each other in a thick silence.

"I'll pick the best," said William. "Nothing but the best for me. Because of the children. A lady. But I am not ready yet. I shan't be ready until the house is built. Then I'll do my searching."

There was a kind of virulence in him, an alien quality which Ursula had never before encountered. She felt a blinding rage against him.

"I wish you good luck," she said distinctly, "though I am sorry for the lady."

Without another word, he turned away from her, and went out of the room. Ursula waited to hear him open and close the vestibule door. But the door neither opened nor shut. She felt him there, in the small closed darkness, as if he were lurking, like some great and inimical beast.

Then she heard his voice. "You don't need to be sorry for the 'lady'," he was saying. "She will know why I am marrying her. She will know there is no sentiment in it." He stopped. "I expect to marry a sensible woman."

"Good night," said Ursula, quietly.

He did not answer. Now he did open the door. He slammed it behind him.

The whole house shook and echoed after that enormous gesture of turbulence. Ursula stood by the fire and listened to it. Her cat came from a corner and rubbed against her skirts. She did not bend and pet it as usual. She continued to gaze at the doorway to the vestibule.

"Why, the horrible man," she said aloud, in a sick, wondering voice. "The horrible, horrible man! He is quite insane. I do hope I'll never see him again."

She would notify Mr. Jenkins tomorrow to see Mr. Prescott. Let Mr. Jenkins take care of the final negotiations. Let him have his commission. It was nothing to her. She could not bear, under any circumstances, to encounter that dreadful man again. It was not to be borne.

The little exquisite house was so still all about her, as still as though a storm had passed over it and it was left alone, safe and quiet from all recent batterings. The lamplight flared; the fire muttered; the cat mewed questioningly. It was a good house, this, but something violent had assaulted it. The violence had gone, without inflicting damage. Life could go on serenely, as usual.

Serene—and empty. Empty as a skull. Full of books and quiet, and empty as death.

CHAPTER II

MR. ALBERT JENKINS sat and beamed humorously at his charming visitor, Ursula Wende. He was a widower. Three years ago he had been relieved of a remarkably repulsive wife, and a year later he had proposed for his old friend's daughter. He had considered himself a catch of no mean attributes; he was one of the richest men in Andersburg, a stockholder in three of the most prosperous mercantile establishments, not to speak of a directorship in the American Lumber Company. He was not yet forty-five, not, he thought, too old for the spinsterish twenty-eight-year-old Ursula. Nor was he physically distasteful to other spinsters, and widows—a short, lean, red-faced little man with a great reputation for amiability and shrewdness. Moreover, he had no children. He also possessed, and lived in, a very handsome home on Crescent Road, a most fashionable and exclusive street. His habits were impeccable; he neither smoked nor drank, nor was he ever heard to utter a word not entirely acceptable in mixed company. The minister of his church regarded him as a most estimable man, which no doubt he was.

Ursula did not consider him a great catch. She did not consider Mr. Jenkins at all, though there was nothing about him to repel a fastidious lady. She had refused him gently, and with a faint surprise. She rather liked him; he was courteous and friendly, and had rescued some of the old Wende fortune for August. But she could not bring herself to think of him as a husband for herself.

She knew him for an avaricious man, who could always "turn a good penny." She did not hold this against him. After all, sensible people liked money, and wanted it; only fools professed a fine scorn for the delightful commodity. So, it was not his avarice, his shrewdness bordering on cunning, which made her refuse him. Once or twice, thinking of her own precarious state, she wondered at her lack of worldly wisdom. But the thought of sharing Mr. Jenkins' house with him, and, candidly, his bed, bored her.

Mr. Jenkins did not become her remorseless enemy because of her lack of sense and her apparent unawareness of what it would mean to be Mrs. Jenkins. He liked Ursula very much. Even though she had refused him, he thought her a young woman of immense distinction and character and good judgment.

Now, as she sat in his office, he thought how superior she was to other ladies of his acquaintanceship. No fussing; no fripperies; no flutterings and aimlessnesses. To be sure, her costume was a little dull, but she gave refinement and gracefulness to it, and extraordinary taste. She was all in brown, from her woolen frock with the white collar, the neat plain cloak, the exquisite gloves, to the bonnet with its inner ruching of tulle, and its brown ribbons. Mr. Jenkins always declared that he disliked ladies who had a streak of the blue stocking in their characters, but, perversely, he liked to talk with Ursula, who understood everything, and never stared vacantly, or protested that all this "legal talk" was quite beyond her delicate mind. Ursula always understood very well.

Ladies of mental power were often "rebels," Mr. Jenkins would think dolorously, licking his late wounds. Mrs. Jenkins had been a "rebel." She had even dared assert, in open company, that women ought to have the right to vote. Only Mr. Jenkins' unassailable position in finance had kept husband and wife on the best calling-lists after that outrage. But Ursula, though a lady of education and intelligence, had no such enormities and peculiarities of character. She never antagonized anyone.

All in all, Ursula would have been perfect as Mrs. Jenkins the second. In the meantime, it was pleasure to see her, and to talk with her. Moreover, gossip never touched her, which was a happy circumstance.

This morning, Ursula had been telling Mr. Jenkins of William Prescott's visit. Naturally, with her customary taste and prudence, she had refrained from imparting all the circumstances. She had only hinted, carefully, that Mr. Prescott had revealed himself to be a most extraordinary man, hasty, savage, impulsive and without a single gentlemanly instinct. She managed to convey all this without the actual words, by a delicate amusement and a wry gesture or two.

"Well, my dear Ursula," he said, leaning back in his chair and beaming at her, "at least you are rid of a most unprofitable piece of land. And at a very good price. You will remember I advised you to sell it for a thousand. But you have sold it for one thousand five hundred. I always considered you a very good businesswoman, you remember."

The cold bright April sunshine struck into the handsome office, with its fire, its leather-covered desk, its good chairs, and its wall of legal books.

Mr. Jenkins surveyed his visitor admiringly. "A very good bargain," he said. "And so Prescott wants to build a house on it, eh? Well, it is just like him, the scoundrel." For a moment, Mr. Jenkins' amiable countenance puckered in an ugly way. "I'm glad you sent him to me for the final details."

"Yes, I wrote him a note, at the Imperial Hotel," said Ursula, without much interest. "I thought the final negotiations had best be conducted by you, Albert."

"A very good thought," admitted Mr. Jenkins, approvingly.

Ursula looked at her gloves.

"It is just like him," repeated Mr. Jenkins, with some sudden passion, "to rush out to you the very night he had seen the property, and demand it. None of those who know him will be in the least surprised."

"Oh," said Ursula, guilelessly, "then he is known in Andersburg?"

"Known!" cried Mr. Jenkins. The chair creaked loudly as he sat up. Now his face showed disgust and repulsion and a black resentment. "Do you mean to say, dear Ursula, that you never heard of him before? Why, *The Clarion* has written about him every week! He is notorious, the rascal!"

"I don't read *The Clarion* often," admitted Ursula. "Papa always got the Pittsburgh and Philadelphia and New York newspapers, and I have kept up the habit. And none of my friends ever mentioned Mr. Prescott to me."

"His name is not fit to be mentioned in decent company!" exclaimed Mr. Jenkins, with great excitement. His sharp red face became almost purple. "A thief and a felon like that! Surely, you can't be unaware of what he did to Arnold, of the American Lumber Company? Why, Arnold was like a father to him. And he ruined Arnold, it is said. I don't know all the details as yet, but *The Clarion* intends to publish the whole nefarious story very soon, and I assure you it will shock Andersburg to its heart."

Mr. Jenkins knew all the details, hence his excitement and his hate-filled voice, loud and harsh in the room. "Ruined Arnold," he repeated. "And it may have terrible consequences for the Company's stockholders." He paused. "Fortunately, I had some hint of this a few months ago, and I may sell out my holdings."

"How clever of you, Albert," murmured Ursula.

"Just a weather eye, my dear Ursula," he said, with an air of self-deprecation. Then he became virtuous and purple again. "But there are a number of my friends who will be involved in this; it is enough to make a man ill."

Ursula gazed at him ingenuously. "How sad that you were not—sure—Albert, a few months ago, and could not tell them what you already guessed, so that they might salvage a little from their investments."

There was a sudden brittle silence in the office. Jenkins stared at Ursula, and his small eyes narrowed.

Ursula's calm gaze remained very candid, and gentle, upon him. An unpleasant thought came to him. He had often remarked to acquaintances that Ursula was "smart as a whip." Why had he said that? Was it some instinct? If she was as smart as he had thought—and he could not just now remember why he had thought it—then she was suspecting something.

He said, almost incoherently: "I—I'm not sure, my dear. It was all

LET LOVE COME LAST

done so undercover by that scoundrel. A feeling, let us say. You ladies would call it intuition." He smiled at her indulgently. She inclined her graceful bonneted head, and smiled back. He breathed easier. "Smart as a whip" some women might be, but, fundamentally, they were all fools. "One does not rush to one's friends without proof, you see——"

Ursula still smiled. All at once, Mr. Jenkins almost disliked her.

"You did not do so badly, yourself," he said, with a rich chuckle. "If you had got five hundred dollars for that slum, I should have congratulated you. But to have got one thousand five hundred——" he spread his hands. "My dear Ursula, you are a financial genius! If you were a man, I should ask you to be my partner, at once! How did you manage to force him to give you all that money?"

Ursula in her reflective voice replied: "Yes, it is a slum, is it not?" She waited, then added, as if making an insignificant remark: "He offered two thousand."

He gaped at her, confounded and incredulous. He could not believe it. He spluttered: "Two thousand? You are not joking? The man must be insane!"

For a few moments Ursula did not answer. She had led a sheltered existence, but she had not been unaware of life. Villainy, through books and hearing and observing, was no new thing to her. She was not disturbed by it. She asked herself, now, very sharply, why she had not been disturbed. Why had she not been made indignant by it, and angered, if not embittered? It is, she thought, only because I have always been so supremely selfish and self-centered, so abominably egotistic.

This man before her was a villain, if only a small and a petty one. Yet she had looked at him and had felt only a faint disdainful amusement. Amusement! She had not known then, but she knew now, that such tolerance could be an evil thing.

She became aware that Albert Jenkins had been laughing incredulously, and that he had said something. She spoke quickly: "Forgive me, Albert, I am afraid my thoughts strayed for a moment. Please, what did you say?"

"I said, it seems impossible that he should have offered you two thousand dollars, and that you should have refused it."

Ursula smiled artlessly. "But, Albert, that would have been dishonest, you see. I knew the land wasn't worth that."

He loved her afresh for this idiocy. "Well," he said, magnanimously, "one thousand five hundred is one thousand too much. I have already made out the deed, after receiving your note. He is to call for it tonight. I understand that he has actually begun operations on the land. No one knew what his intention was. You tell me he wishes to build a house. Right next door to chicken coops and shacks and stony fields! Well, well!"

"I wonder why he wanted that land?" asked Ursula.

Mr. Jenkins scowled. "I'll tell you why! Because nobody, after hearing the—rumors—and knowing what he was, would sell him a single clod of earth anywhere!"

"He tried to buy land somewhere else?"

Mr. Jenkins frowned again, and rubbed his chin. "Well, I can't just say. Not for sure. Never heard of it." He became thoughtful, and stared into space. "Now why should Prescott buy that particular piece of land? Very strange."

Ursula smoothed her gloves. "Andersburg can't move farther east, because that is the industrial section, where all those factories and mills are, and no one would care for that, and good land beyond that area is too far from the city. It can't move north, because the hills are there, like a barrier, and most of the land is in estates. It can't move south, because of the river, and the docks, and the farms nearby. So it seems odd to me that no one ever thought that it might move west. I suppose that is because Andersburg hasn't grown much recently. But if it should suddenly start to grow, the west is the only place, isn't it?"

If Ursula had been a man, Mr. Jenkins would have sworn suddenly and violently, and would have called himself an idiot, and his friends also. Of course, it was obvious! Just because Andersburg had hardly grown since the war was no reason why it shouldn't do so now. Of course, the farmers along the river and slightly inland would eventually be induced, by high offers, to sell the land for suburban or city development. But the prices would indeed be high! To the west, however, the stony and undesirable land lay, cheap and unwanted, waiting only for a clever man to buy it, or a group of clever men of vision, anticipating the future. One could buy all the land one wished, from the miserable squatters and grubby truck-gardeners and artisans who lived there——

Mr. Jenkins dropped his eyelids, to conceal the sudden sharp gleam in his eye. It was an instinctive gesture, even before Ursula, who could not possibly understand such things as speculation in land. Mr. Jenkins' heart began to beat very fast. The suburbs, the desirable ones, were already becoming crowded.

Then he had a sickening thought. Someone had already thought of all this. William Prescott. It was to be expected. William Prescott, ugly rat from Clifton Street, despoiler of better men, thief and liar and conniver and scoundrel! Mr. Jenkins stammered, watching Ursula closely:

"Did Prescott mention buying any other land in that vicinity?"

Ursula knew very well what was transpiring in Mr. Jenkins' mind. Her old habit of faint amusement tried to assert itself. Instead, and she felt this with a kind of exhilaration, contempt came to her, clear and vivid.

She said, as if in vague wonder: "No. But then, our interview was very short, really. I found him most disagreeable. We concluded our arrangements, and he left."

Suddenly, she remembered him beside her, at her desk. She saw the spill shaking in his hard brown hand. That hand became intensely visible to her now, in the light of the remembered sudden flare of the lamp.

She heard Mr. Jenkins sigh with relief. He had taken up a pen. He was tapping it thoughtfully against his teeth. He said, quite loudly: "It was only because he could not buy elsewhere."

Ursula's shoulders moved under her cloak in something like a shrug. She wanted to go. But the thing, the obscure but powerful impulse which had brought her to this office today, held her in her chair.

"I suppose you are right, dear Albert," she said, encouragingly. She paused. "A most uncivil man, Mr. Prescott. And, from what you have told me, apparently disreputable. Odd, too."

"Insane," agreed Mr. Jenkins, emphatically. "Do you know what he did a year ago? He adopted a brat left in a slum hallway by some slut, some unknown female, of whom the less said, in the presence of a lady like yourself, the better. The brat was about a year old, then. Origin unknown," said Mr. Jenkins, using legal phraseology. "The orphan asylum is very crowded and wretched, so he had no difficulty. It was in the papers. Made quite a stir. Everyone laughed at him, and properly, too. But now the wretch has a nursemaid for the brat, and has rented the best suite in the Imperial Hotel. And he is paying a pretty penny for it, too!" Mr. Jenkins chuckled enviously, thinking of his friend, the owner and proprietor of the hotel. "Well, dishonestly come, easily go, to paraphrase the old saying about money," he added.

"He is a rich man?" asked Ursula, innocently.

Mr. Jenkins bristled. "No one knows! He doesn't bank here, or I'd know from Bassett. Banks in Pittsburgh. Probably not, though he will be," he added, with a return of his original infuriated malignance. "But I do know this: someone is backing him, to the extreme limit. And I know who the 'someone' is. An outsider."

Ursula appeared bewildered, and Mr. Jenkins did not enlarge.

"It was a kind thing, at least, to adopt the child," she murmured.

Mr. Jenkins laughed shortly. He was about to make an insinuating remark, but refrained, remembering his visitor's sex. He said: "I told you he was insane. Do you know what else he did, a week ago? He gave the orphanage five thousand dollars, for a new wing!"

Ursula's wine-colored eyes became very bright and intent, as they regarded Mr. Jenkins. Suddenly, without knowing why, he flushed sullenly.

"I suppose," he said, with elaborate carelessness, "there are some who would approve of that. I, myself, think he intends a strong attack on Andersburg society in the near future; he believes he will ingratiate himself this way. He will be sadly disillusioned, I am sure. No one worth anything, socially, will ever have anything to do with Bill Prescott, even if he endows a college or a dozen orphan asylums. We know him too well for what he is, and when the whole story comes out he will be more anathema than ever—the trash!"

"But why, until the story is known, is he held in such low esteem?" asked Ursula.

Mr. Jenkins became quite excited. "My dear Ursula! Who *is* the man? The son of a woman who kept a noisome house for the workers in the mills and factories! A man who is nobody! An upstart, a climber, from the slums! A former waiter, if not worse! He hasn't a friend in the city! No schooling, nothing——"

"He speaks like an educated man, if he does not have an educated man's careful accent," said the daughter of a schoolmaster.

Mr. Jenkins shrugged. "There is some rumor that old Cowlesbury— that ancient quack doctor who died about ten years ago—took an interest in him, let him read his books, bought him books, actually, and tutored him in his spare time. But everyone knew about Cowlesbury. He was more than a little mad, himself, living off there in the woods, after his retirement, with a pack of dogs. He had about two thousand dollars when he died, and he left it—with all his books—to Prescott."

Ursula vaguely remembered Dr. Cowlesbury, who had been a town "character" for many years. He must have been almost a hundred years old when he had died. Whatever esteem or position he had ever commanded had been forgotten twenty years before his death. Ursula had never seen him, but had sometimes heard his name mentioned.

She rose, and Mr. Jenkins came to his feet with gallant alacrity.

"My dear Ursula," he said, grateful that she was leaving, so that